Jack and Lily

Jack and Lily

Angela McAllister
illustrated by Phillida Gili

Orion
Children's Books

for Luke and Eleanor
and in memory of their wonderful Grandad
A.M.

First published in Great Britain in 2001
by Orion Children's Books
a division of the Orion Publishing Group Ltd
Orion House
5 Upper St Martin's Lane
London WC2H 9EA

Text copyright © Angela McAllister 2001
Illustrations copyright © Phillida Gili 2001
Designed by Louise Millar
The right of Angela McAllister and Phillida Gili to be identified
as author and illustrator of this work has been asserted.

A catalogue record for this book is available from the British Library

Printed in Italy by Printer Trento S.r.l.

Contents

CONTENTS

Lost and Found

Jack was looking for something he had lost.

He hunted through the toy basket in the sitting room but it wasn't there. He stretched up to look on the mantelpiece, where Mum kept her best china cats, but it wasn't there either. He looked under the cushion of the window seat, but he only found a crayon and a comb.

Jack went out into the hall and began to look in his coat pockets.

Lily came along, pushing her wooden horse. She thought Jack was going out somewhere.

"Me out too!" she said and sat down to put her boots on.

In the hall there was always a jumble of shoes and sandals and welly boots. Lily pulled on a small left boot and a middle-size left boot.

She didn't mind.

"We're not going out now," said Jack, but Lily followed him, just in case . . .

Jack went
along the hall to the
cupboard under the stairs.

He looked inside. He could see
Dad's sports bag, the paddling pool,
torches and candles, the cat basket,
umbrellas and raincoats.

Right at the back was a warm, dark
secret place. Jack loved its smell of polish
and suitcases.

He crept inside. He found a fire
engine but he wasn't looking for a fire engine.
And then as he tried to crawl out he met Lily trying
to crawl in. Jack roared one of his tiger roars and Lily
scrambled out again in a hurry.

Next Jack decided to look in his bedroom. Halfway up the stairs was his special thinking place. If he sat on this stair he could see out of the little window above the front door, right across the street, where Mum's friend Penny lived.

Over the rooftops he could see the trees in the park and the tower at the fire station where the firemen hung their hoses to dry.

Jack often sat on this step. He liked being not quite up and not quite down, and not quite in and not quite out. But today he didn't stop. He stomped up the stairs with a frown on his face.

He went up to the top and into Mum and Dad's bedroom. Sometimes, if Jack woke up early, he would take his toys into their bedroom and play on the rug beside the bed until their alarm clock went off.

Sure enough, there on the rug were Jack's cars all parked in a line, just as he'd left them that morning. But he wasn't looking for a car.

Lily came up the stairs, singing *'Three blind mice'*, but her words were all nonsense. When she saw Jack in Mum and Dad's room she went in. Lily stood in front of the long mirror and smiled at herself. Then she leant forward and kissed her reflection!

Jack picked up one of Mum's earrings from her dressing table and held it in his hand, carefully, as if it was real treasure. It smelt of delicious perfume. Then he heard Mum start to sing along to the radio downstairs in the kitchen.

"Come on Lily," he whispered. "We shouldn't be in here, let's look in my bedroom."

"Me look too," said Lily, although she didn't know what they were looking for. She was just happy that Jack wanted her to play with him.

Jack wriggled under his bed and pulled out his toy boxes. He tipped the box of animals out onto the rug but the lost thing wasn't there. Lily picked up a picture book and climbed into the empty box.

Then Jack put his hand into the jigsaw box and felt around, but the lost thing wasn't there either. It wasn't up on his shelf with the treasures that Lily wasn't allowed to touch.

It wasn't in the old shoebox where he kept interesting stones and shells. It wasn't in the pocket of his dressing gown. Where else could he look?

Just at that moment Jack noticed Lily quietly going off with a piece of jigsaw in her hand. He had a thought. Maybe Lily had hidden the lost thing so he followed her. Lily went downstairs, bumping slowly on her bottom.

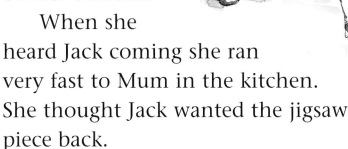

When she heard Jack coming she ran very fast to Mum in the kitchen. She thought Jack wanted the jigsaw piece back.

"What's up!" said Mum as Jack and Lily raced through the door together.

"I've lost something and I think Lily's hidden it," said Jack. Lily kept the jigsaw piece behind her back.

"Mine!" she said and held onto Mum's leg tightly.

"What have you lost?" asked Mum.

"That little magnifying glass with the red handle that Grandad gave me," said Jack.

"Oh dear," said Mum. "I can't remember where that is."

Lily let go of Mum's leg.

"There," she said, holding out the piece of jigsaw.

Jack shook his head. "No, Lily, that's not what I'm looking for."

But Lily just pointed the piece of jigsaw at Jack.

"There," she said. "There!"

Suddenly Mum laughed. She had seen what Lily had seen. "There," she said just like Lily, "in your trouser pocket."

Jack put his hand into his pocket and sure enough there was the magnifying glass. It had been following him about all the time. The hunt was over.

Lily knew she had done something clever. Mum gave her a big hug.

"You see, little sisters can be useful sometimes," said Mum.

But Jack was already running upstairs to the bathroom with his magnifying glass, to find out exactly how many legs a spider really has.

Lily's Pet

Lily was playing in the sandpit.

She was very busy burying fir cones in the sand and then digging them out again.

Suddenly she noticed something. A snail had crept onto the edge of the sandpit. Lily dropped her spade and jumped up.

"No, no, no!" she said. But she didn't run away.

The snail stretched out its head and swayed from side to side. It had two long horns and two short ones. It waved them gently.

Lily crouched down to have a closer look. The snail's curly shell was stripy like Grandad's cough sweets. Lily touched it. The snail pulled its head quickly into the shell to hide.

"No, no, no!" said Lily again. She lay down on her tummy and tried to see inside the shell. After a moment the snail came out to look at her. Its skin was wrinkly. Lily didn't want to touch that.

The snail began to move slowly. It crept over a piece of leaf and round a drop of water. Lily spooned a little mound of sand in front of it, but the snail didn't like that. It turned and started to go down the side of the sandpit. Lily didn't want the snail to go away.

She scrambled to her feet and ran inside.

No one noticed Lily run into the house in her wet welly boots. She didn't pull them off at the back door as she was supposed to. She ran straight to the toy basket in the sitting room and started to hunt for something. When she'd found what she wanted Lily ran out again. In her hand she had a tiny dog basket from the doll's house.

But when Lily got into the garden the snail had gone. It wasn't on the side of the sandpit, and it wasn't in the grass. Only a slimy trail showed where it had been. Lily followed the shiny path carefully with her finger, but it stopped at the edge of the sandpit.

"All gone," said Lily, looking around her. "All gone, all gone."

So she picked up her spade and buried the little dog basket in the sand . . . And then she dug it up again.

Jack and Lily and the Dog

It was a sunny morning so Jack and Lily were playing in the garden. Jack wanted to play football. But Lily wanted to play chase. Every time Jack kicked the ball Lily picked it up and ran off with it.

"Throw the ball back, Lily," said Jack.

But Lily just hugged it tighter.

Jack looked around for another ball and found one in the flowerbed. He kicked that. Lily dropped the first ball and ran away with the second one. Each time Jack kicked one Lily ran after it. It was quite a good game but not as good as proper football.

When Mum came out with some biscuits and milk Jack said "I wish Lily was big enough to kick the ball back to me."

Mum gave him a hug. "I know it's difficult sometimes with a little sister. One day she'll be able to do everything that you can."

"But then she might not *want* to do the same as me," said Jack.

They looked at Lily who was trying very hard to sit on the football and kept tumbling off.

"You're probably right," said Mum with a sigh and a smile. "She does seem to have some funny ideas of her own."

Then Mum said "Let's go to the park. We can take the ball with us and bread for the ducks."

So Mum packed some drinks and sandwiches in a bag and put Lily in the pushchair. Jack found the sunhats and off they went to the park. Jack carried the ball all the way.

Jack and Lily's park was just a short walk from their house. When Mum opened the park gate Lily undid her harness and climbed out of the pushchair.

She ran with Jack to the playground. Jack always got there first and went straight to the slide. He was big enough to go on the highest one by himself.

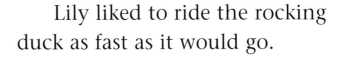

Lily liked to ride the rocking duck as fast as it would go.

"Come on, Lily," called Jack. "Come and find me."

He slid down the slide and climbed up into the wooden castle. Lily slipped off the duck and followed him.

Mum sat on the bench and tried to remember what shopping she needed to buy on the way home.

She didn't notice a little dog appear.

The little dog scampered after Lily and went into the castle. All of a sudden Mum heard lots of barking and giggling.

Jack came out of a tunnel, Lily crawled out behind him and then the little dog shot out and ran round and round chasing its tail.

"Hello!" said Mum in surprise. "You're not supposed to be in here." She looked around for the dog's owner. "Is this your dog?" she asked some people walking by, but they shook their heads.

The little dog was very friendly.

"Can't we play with him?" asked Jack. "I think he likes us."

Mum shook her head. "The sign at the gate says '*No Dogs allowed in the playground*'," she said. "And besides, someone may be looking for him."

Mum picked up the dog and lifted him over the gate.

"Off you go," she said. But the little dog just sat still, put its head to one side and looked at them.

"Go on, off you go. Go home," said Mum.

Jack could see that Mum was trying to look serious but her face really wanted to smile. She looked like that sometimes when she was talking to Lily.

"He is a lovely dog," she said, "but he should go home."

But the little dog didn't go home.

By the time Mum had lifted Lily onto the seesaw the little dog was back again, sniffing the sandwich bag.

"Come on little dog," called Jack. "Come and find me."

This time Jack climbed into the castle, crossed the rope bridge, went up the ramp to the tower and down the fireman's pole. The little dog followed. He stopped at the fireman's pole and looked for Jack. Then he turned around and ran very fast back down the steps. Lily squealed with delight.

"Oh dear," said Mum. "He must have got in through a hole in the hedge somewhere. We'll have to catch him."

Jack and Mum chased the little dog round and round the playground. The little dog thought it was a game. He ran much too fast to be caught.

"I give up," gasped Mum. "Maybe we'd better go and feed the ducks. I'm sure he will follow us or go home."

So they went down to the stream. The little dog sniffed at the trees along the way.

"He's pretending that he isn't following us," said Jack. "I love that dog."

But when Jack and Lily started to throw bread to the ducks the little dog came charging up and jumped into the water with a huge splash. The ducks flew away quacking.

"Dog swimmin'," said Lily and she sat down and started to take her sandals off. She wanted to swim too.

Suddenly a voice called out, "Biggles! Biggles!"

Jack saw a boy and a big girl walking across the grass. The little dog ran to them as fast as it could, wagging his tail and barking.

"This must be your dog," said Mum. "I'm glad he's found you."

Biggles jumped up at the girl, yapping excitedly.

"It's all right," she said. "We live next door to the park. Biggles often runs off looking for an adventure but we know where to find him."

Jack noticed that the boy was carrying a football.

"Are you going to play?" he asked.

"Yes," said the boy.

"Do you want to play with us?"

Jack looked at Mum.

"Of course you can," she said.

The big girl was called Patty and her brother was called Sam. Sam put a lead on the little dog and tied him to the goal post. "Biggles is the goalie," he said.

While Jack played football with his new friends, Lily chased Mum in and out of the trees. After the game they all shared the sandwiches and squash.

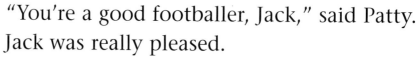

"You're a good footballer, Jack," said Patty. Jack was really pleased.

When it was time to say goodbye Jack gave Biggles a big hug.

"I think he likes you," said Sam.

"Can we play with him again?" said Jack.

"Yes," said Mum, packing up the picnic. "If it's sunny tomorrow we'll come back after lunch."

"See you tomorrow, then," said Patty and she threw a stick towards home for Biggles.

Lily climbed into the pushchair and yawned. Jack strapped her in. "You're a good chaser, Lily," he said kindly, giving her the ball to hold. Lily smiled, then Jack pushed his sleepy sister all the way home.

Lily Helps Out

Jack and Lily were in Mum's bedroom helping her sort out some of their old clothes for a jumble sale.

"You are growing so fast, Jack," said Mum as she heaped the things on her bed. "All these winter clothes will be much too small for you next year."

"Me small," said Lily. She tugged a jumper out of the pile and pulled it over her head.

"Yes, you're small," said Mum with a laugh. "But these are boys clothes."

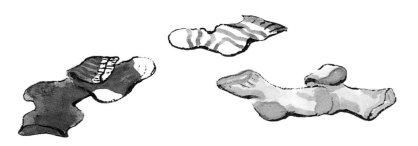
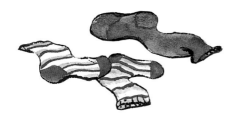

Jack put on his old coat. His arms stuck out of the sleeves and made him look like a scarecrow. So he put on Mum's straw hat and stood on one leg.

"Can't we keep them for dressing up?" he asked, with a wobble.

"It would be fun to have a dressing up box," said Mum. "Why don't we look for some useful things at the jumble sale on Saturday?"

"We could use the box we brought back from the supermarket," said Jack and he went off to find it.

Meanwhile Lily was busy pulling some of the clothes off the bed to make a nest on the floor.

Mittens, the kitten, came upstairs to see what was going on. When she saw Lily's nest she stepped right inside, curled up and went to sleep.

"Night, night," whispered Lily, and she covered Mittens up with the straw hat.

Just then the doorbell rang. It was Mum's friend Penny. She had come to collect the jumble.

"There was much more than I thought," said Mum. "We haven't quite finished yet. You go up to the bedroom and I'll fetch some bags to put everything in."

A moment later Penny called from the top of the stairs.

"I don't think you'll need those bags. These clothes are going to walk to my car by themselves."

Mum and Jack and Lily peered around the bedroom door.

They saw the straw hat creep across the carpet, pulling a pair of old leggings and a long sock behind it. Suddenly it stopped, bobbed up and down, and scuttled under the bed. Whatever could be happening?

"Mittens night night," said Lily.

"Mittens wake up!" said Jack.

Soon it was Saturday, the day of the jumble sale. Jack, Lily and Mum went to the church hall early, but a queue of people was already waiting. When the doors were opened everyone pushed inside.

Around the hall were tables piled with things; jugs and saucepans, books, paintings, clothes and all sorts of bits and pieces. There was even a bicycle and a guitar.

"I'm going to have a rummage," said Mum.

Jack didn't know what a *rummage* was. It sounded like the sort of thing you ate with a cup of tea. He hoped he was going to get one too.

First Mum found a red velvet curtain.

"This would make a wonderful cloak," she said. "You could dress up as a king, Jack."

Jack had a better idea.

"Lily could be Red Riding Hood," he said, "and I could be the wolf!"

He roared at Lily and showed his claws.

One of the jumble sale ladies gave him a cross look, so he roared again, even louder.

At the next table Mum bought some old bracelets and necklaces. Jack found a spotted hankie just like a pirate's.

"It's got a pirate smell," he said, so they had that too. Before long they had a bag of hats and clothes for the dressing up box.

Mum saw a bundle of old magazines. "I think we'll buy these to decorate our box," she said. "We can do it this afternoon when we get home."

While she was paying Jack noticed some other interesting things under the tables. He was just crawling underneath to have a look when Lily came up behind him and roared her loudest roar. Jack sat up and bumped his head!

"Me tiger," said Lily and she showed him a stripy scarf tucked into her trousers for a tail.

"Well, that's another thing for the box," said Mum.
She took her purse out of her bag again.
"Are you looking for dressing-up clothes?" asked the jumble sale lady. She bent down to talk to Lily. "Come and see what I have here."

Lily held the lady's hand and followed her into the back room. Then she came out again wearing a pair of sparkly fairy wings!

"Someone brought these in this morning and I haven't had a chance to hang them up," said the lady. "I was waiting for a little girl to come along."

Mum smiled at Lily. For one moment she looked just like an angel. Then Lily stretched out her arms as if she was going to fly . . . tripped over and fell on her nose!

"I think you need flying lessons," said Jack and he helped her up. Lily rubbed her dusty hands on her trousers and gave Jack a hug. So Mum bought the fairy wings too.

On the way home they met Mum's friend Penny who showed them a silver handbag she'd bought.

"Did you enjoy the jumble sale?" she asked Jack.

Jack thought hard for a moment. "No, and yes," he said. "Mum didn't give me a *rummage,* but we did get a real pirate's hankie."

When they got home, Mum buttered some rolls for
lunch while Jack and Lily looked at the magazines.

"See if you can find any pictures to decorate
our dressing-up box," Mum said.

Jack and Lily found a picture of

a footballer

a magician

a clown

a swimmer

and a ballet dancer.

Jack tore each useful page out.

After lunch Mum mixed up some white powder paint in an old ice cream tub.

"First we'll paint the box," she said. "But before we start let's get your aprons and some newspaper to put on the floor."

Mum and Jack went to fetch the aprons and paper. Lily was left all on her own. She went and sat beside the ice cream tub. Then do you know what she did? Lily picked up the brush and started to paint the box white. The brush dripped everywhere so she painted the floor too. Then she noticed there were splashes on her trousers so she painted herself all over.

When Jack came into the kitchen Lily smiled at him like a happy ghost.

"Oh no! Mum," shouted Jack, "come and see..."

Mum came and saw. She sighed her *'What-have-you-done-now-Lily?'* sigh. She took off Lily's trousers, socks and shoes and tickled her all the way to the bathroom.

When everything was cleaned up Mum gave Lily a carrot to eat while she and Jack finished painting the box. Jack cut out the pictures and glued them on.

Then Mum found a packet of stars for Lily to stick on. "Now it really looks like a dressing-up box," said Jack.

At last it was time to put the clothes into the box. "Be good, Lily, while I go upstairs to fetch the things," said Mum.

Lily wanted to cut something out but she couldn't use the scissors properly. "It's all done, Lily," said Jack. "There isn't room for any more now."

But Lily took one of the magazines. While Mum and Jack bundled the clothes into the box Lily tore out a picture. She pasted it with glue and stuck it onto the box.

"Very good, Lily," said Mum when she saw the picture of a black and white cat. "But it's a dressing-up box, not a cat basket."

Lily smiled a secret smile. She leaned into the box and started pulling all the clothes out again. Before Mum could stop her, two furry ears, two green eyes and a pink whiskery nose peeped over the top.

"Cat basket!" said Lily.

"Meeeow!" said Mittens with a yawn, and she snuggled down in the box again to go back to sleep.

Friends

Jack and Dad were walking to the corner shop to buy some milk. A man and a boy came along the street towards them.

"Hello there!" said the man to Jack's dad.

"Hello Harry," said Dad. They stopped to have a chat.

While they were talking Jack looked at the boy and the boy looked at him.

"I'm five," said the boy.

"I'm four and a half," said Jack.

"I've got a stone," said the boy. He took a stone out of his trouser pocket and showed it to Jack. It was round and white with a black spot in the middle.

"It's an eye stone," said the boy. "Do you want to hold it?"

Jack took the stone and turned it over in his hand. It did look just like an eye.

"Can it see us?" asked Jack.

"Yes," said the boy, "and it can see in the dark."

"Where did you get it from?" asked Jack.

"My garden," the boy replied.

"I've got a garden," said Jack.

"Maybe you can find one then," said the boy.

"I've got a tiger at the bottom of my garden, said Jack. "In the bushes."

"I've got a tiger in my garden too!" said the boy. "I like tigers."

Jack liked this boy who liked tigers.

"My tiger eats rabbits and foxes."

"My tiger can climb trees."

"My tiger eats burglars."

"And jumps right
over the house."

"And gives me a ride on its back."

"And roars as loud as thunder!"

"Tigers are my favourite," said Jack.

"Yes," said the boy. "And stones . . ." He looked at his stone again."Would you like to keep it? I know I can find another one. It's easy."

Jack took the stone. He felt very proud that the boy wanted to give it to him. "Thank you," he said."I'll keep it in my treasure box."

Then Jack's dad shook hands with his friend.

"See you around," said Harry.

"Yup," said Dad. "See you around."

The boy smiled at Jack. "See you around," he said and stuck his thumb up.

Jack stuck his thumb up too. "Yup," he said. "See you around."

Dad and Jack went on their way to the shop.

"I used to work with that man," said Dad. "We're friends."

Jack turned the stone over and over in his pocket.

"That boy is five and he gave me a stone with an eye that can see in the dark, and he's got a tiger in his garden that eats burglars," he said. "We're friends too."

"That's nice," said Dad with a smile, and he took hold of Jack's hand as they walked along. "It's good to have a friend."

Thursday Afternoons

Every Thursday Jack and Lily spent the afternoon at Grandma and Grandad's house while Mum went shopping. They loved going to Grandma and Grandad's house. They always had fun there.

Grandma and Grandad lived nearby. Mum took Jack and Lily along after lunch.

When they arrived Jack knocked loudly on the door and stretched up to ring the bell. Grandad called out,

"No thank you, we don't want any today."

Jack squealed with laughter and Lily got excited and laughed too.

"It's me, Grandad," yelled Jack. "It's Jack and Lily!"

They both knocked on the door and peeped through the letter box.

Grandad opened the door. "Hello, my little cauliflowers," he said with a grin, "come on in."

"See you later," said Mum. "Be good." But they had already run into the garden to find Grandma.

Grandma and Grandad's garden was full of tall plants and bushes with little paths winding in between. Lily followed Jack.

"Grandma," they called, "where are you?"

She was at the end of the garden in her greenhouse, filling tiny flowerpots with earth. Jack and Lily ran in and gave her a hug. They all got covered with earth.

"Hello, you two!" said Grandma.

Jack rubbed his hands on his trousers, pulled a piece of paper out of his pocket and gave it to Grandma.

"I did this drawing for you," he said. It was a picture of Grandma's house.

"How clever of you to get the right number of windows, Jack," said Grandma. She peered closely at the drawing. "What is this thing on the roof? Is it a big chimney?"

"No," said Jack. "It's a rocket in case you want to go up to the moon or something."

"That's very useful," said Grandma. "We might zoom up there later to get something from the moon for tea."

"Tea!" said Lily at the top of her voice. "Tea, tea!"

Lily said 'tea' whenever she wanted something to eat.

"It's not tea time yet," Grandma said laughing. She picked Lily up and gave her a cuddle.

"Oh, Lily, why do you always smell of strawberry jam?" she said.

"It does feel like biscuit time," said Jack in his special *'I'm-being-good-and-not-asking-but-just-suggesting'* sort of voice.

"Come on, then," said Grandma. "Let's go and get cleaned up."

After biscuits, Grandad asked Jack to help him feed the goldfish in the pond. Grandma took Lily upstairs.

Going upstairs with Lily took quite a long time in Grandma's house. The wall up the stairs was covered with photographs. Lily always pointed to each one and Grandma had to say who it was.

"That's Uncle George, that's Uncle Patrick and his dog Betsy. That's Mummy when she was a little girl, and that's Grandad when he had a funny moustache."

Sometimes Lily would say "again!" and wriggle about in Grandma's arms until Grandma took her downstairs and started right from the beginning again.

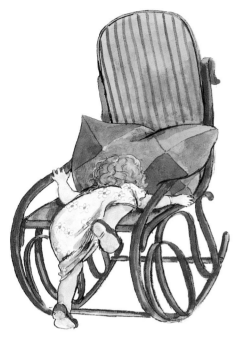

Up in the bedroom was a rocking chair. It had big cushions that Grandma had sewn herself. Lily ran to the chair and tried to climb on.

"Shall I help you?" said Grandma, but Lily said "No, no, no!" very firmly.

She wanted to get up all by herself. Lily lifted her foot high, the chair rocked forward and she fell over. But Grandma didn't pick her up, she could see that Lily was trying to be a big girl.

Lily got up and tried again. This time she got her foot on the chair. She grabbed at the cushions, but they just slid across the seat and she fell off again. "Hold onto the arm of the chair, Lily," said Grandma, tapping the arm to show her where. Lily pushed Grandma's hand away and tried again. She lifted her leg, held on tight and scrambled up. She was trying so hard that her face went red. But at last she managed to pull herself up, turn around and sit down.

"Well done, clever girl!" said Grandma and made a big fuss.

Lily was very pleased with herself. "Up," she said. "Me up!" But instead of sitting back and having a rest in the rocking chair, do you know what she did? She slid off and tried to do it all over again.

49

After that Grandma and Lily made some shortbread and Lily helped Grandma wash up at the sink. She loved to stir the bubbly water with a wooden spoon and pour it through the sieve.

Jack and Grandad came in from the garden. Grandad sat down on the back doorstep to take off his old gardening boots. Jack helped to pull the boots off.

"When I grow up I'm going to marry you, Grandad," said Jack as he tugged with all his might.

"Well, you'll have to wash my smelly socks then," said Grandad with a wink and the boots came off with a bump.

"Teatime," called Grandma.

She had set the table with Jack and Lily's own special cups and plates. There were sandwiches and cake and the warm crumbly shortbread. Lily was standing on a chair and had already helped herself.

"Actually this isn't an ordinary cake, you know," said Grandma as she poured the tea. "Lily and I went up to the moon in our rocket and brought it back while you were in the garden."

Grandad looked puzzled. "Mooncake, eh?" he said.

Grandma showed him Jack's picture and Jack explained about the rocket on the roof.

Just then the doorbell rang. "That'll be your mum," said Grandad. Grandma got up to put the kettle on.

"Quick, Lily," said Jack. He helped her climb out of her chair.

But they didn't rush into the hall to say hello to Mum. Do you know what they did? Jack opened the back door and they ran up the garden path and hid in the shed, giggling together – just as they did every Thursday!

And why did they do that? Because Jack and Lily always had such a wonderful time at Grandma and Grandad's house that they never wanted to go home!

Jack and Lily's Bath

It was raining and Jack couldn't go out to play. "I don't know what to do," he said to Mum.

"I've got just the thing for a rainy day," said Mum, and she fetched the face paints that Grandma had given Jack for his birthday. Jack had forgotten all about them.

"I want to be a tiger," he said. Tigers were Jack's favourite animal. Mum painted his face orange with black stripes and whiskers.

He sat as still as a statue while she put the paint on so there were no smudges. When he looked in the mirror he was very pleased. "Grrrrragh!!" Jack growled and went off to make a den in the cupboard under the stairs.

Lily was having her morning nap but the sound of the growling tiger woke her up.

"Oh dear," sighed Mum. "I thought I might have a quiet cup of coffee while Lily was asleep. Never mind."

Mum got Lily up. When Lily saw the brush and colours she wanted her face painted too. She tugged Mum's skirt.

"Me cat, me cat!" she said.

"I'll give you black and white stripes," said Mum. But Lily couldn't keep still. She scrunched up her nose. Mum did her best.

"You need some whiskers, little cat," she said, "and then you can go off and hunt for a mouse."

But just then a fierce tiger leapt into the kitchen and roared "GRRRRRRRRAGH!!" Lily turned round and her whiskers went all wobbly right up to her ear!

"Oh well," said Mum, "you can be the cat with the crumpled whiskers, just like the cow with the crumpled horn in the nursery rhyme."

Jack and Lily played Tiger and Cat all day. They found scarf tails in the dressing up box and had fish cakes in the shape of little fishes for lunch.

"Cats like fish, so I expect tigers do too," said Mum.

"Tigers are big cats so they like more," said Jack, wiping some ketchup off his whiskers.

In the afternoon the sun came out and they played creeping and pouncing in the garden jungle. By the end of the day Tiger and Cat had rubbed off their whiskers altogether. Their beautiful painted faces had been smudged and smeared and nearly wiped away. Mum looked at them. "It's definitely time for a bath!" she said.

Jack and Lily loved having a bath so they went up to the bathroom, still growling. (Lily had been a growling cat all day because purring was too difficult.)

Mum fetched their pyjamas and slippers.

In the bathroom Jack had a stool to stand on to help him reach the taps and toothbrushes. That meant he could wash his hands and brush his teeth by himself, although Mum always gave his teeth an extra brush for luck.

Lily liked Jack's stool. She often carried it about and sat on the stool in different places, or climbed on it to reach things she wanted – especially Jack's crocodile toothbrush.

Mum ran the bathwater. Then she helped Jack out of his jumper. And do you know what Lily did?

She climbed onto the stool and stirred the water with the crocodile toothbrush. As it got deeper she paddled her hands in the bubbles.

"Oh no!" said Mum when she turned round. There was a big bubbly puddle on the bathmat. Mum sighed her *'What-have-you-done-now,–Lily!'* sigh. Lily stamped on the bubbles and laughed.

"I can't take my eyes off you for a minute!" said Mum, mopping up the mess. Lily started to undo the sticky straps of her shoes but she couldn't undress herself, so Mum helped. Then she put Lily in the bath while Jack used his stool to climb in.

Jack and Lily sat among the bobbing bath toys. There were whales with water spouts, ducks and little boats. There were old bubble bath bottles of different shapes and sizes. Lily poured water from her favourite bottle into a cup and then a plastic sieve to make rain. Jack filled up the big bottle and squirted Lily's tummy. Lily squealed and tipped her cup over Jack's head. Mum spread a big towel on the floor to catch the splashes.

While Jack and Lily were playing they didn't notice their wet painted faces dripping colours into the bathwater. After a while all that was left of Tiger and Cat was a smudge on Jack's forehead and a smear on Lily's cheek.

Mum folded up the clothes and had a tidy around the bathroom while they were busy.

Then Lily decided to stand up. She had a sponge in each hand and held them high above her head. She squeezed them hard. Water splashed down like a waterfall. "Aaaaaah!" she said loudly. It was her favourite game. Sometimes she said "Eeeeee" and sometimes she said "Ooooo", but she always said it loudly and Jack joined in. Mum put her hands over her ears.

Next Jack made cups of magic drink with bubbles on top. Mum pretended to drink hers. "Mmm, champagne," she said. "It makes you giggle." But Lily really did drink hers, even though the water was a very dirty colour!

Mum decided it was time to do some washing. She scrubbed away the smudges of face paint. Jack liked having his hair washed, but Lily didn't like hairwashing at all. She wouldn't look up and she wouldn't shut her eyes, so Mum had to use a special hat that kept the soap out of Lily's eyes. She looked at Lily in the hat and smiled.

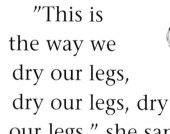

"You look like an angel with a halo," she said, kissing her on the nose. "But I don't think an angel would soak my bathroom floor!"

At last it was time to get out.

Lily wanted to stay in the bath until all the water had gone. "More, Mummy, more," she said, but Mum fished her out and began to sing.

"This is the way we dry our legs, dry our legs, dry our legs," she sang, and Lily kicked her legs and chewed the towel.

Jack got dry all by himself.

Once they were in their dressing-gowns with their hair dry, Jack and Lily were ready for stories. Dad came home just in time to read to them.

"What have you done today, you two?" he asked as they both squeezed onto his lap.

Jack yawned and shook his head. "I can't remember," he said, hugging his second-best tiger. But Lily remembered it all. She lifted her hands above her head and scrunched up her nose. "Me cat, rrrrragh, bath, angel!" she told him.

"And are you going to be a cat or an angel tomorrow?" asked Dad.

For a moment Lily looked at Dad with a sleepy angel's face . . . then she roared a loud "GRRRRRAGH!"

Sofa Mountain

Jack was playing with his cars on the sofa. He drove them up one arm of the sofa, all along the straight road at the back and down the other arm. Then he drove them around the bumpy cushions.

"This is the rocky mountain," he said to himself in his important-playing-voice. "Watch out for breakdowns." He fetched a breakdown lorry from the toy basket and parked it in a cushion cave. Then he filled another lorry with some toy animals and drove it across the carpet to the sofa. "Make way," he said in a different voice. "We're moving our zoo over the mountain."

Jack's zoo animals climbed over the rocky mountains. Elephant found a zip on the cushion cover.

"Let's sleep in here," Jack said in his elephant voice. He unzipped the cushion cover and made the animals climb inside.

A red sports car zoomed down the sofa mountain.

"Burglars are coming!" said Jack. "Who's the guard?" He pulled out the lion cub and made him leap about.

"I'm fierce," he said. "I'll be the guard. Rrrragh!"

But the red sports car zoomed faster and faster and knocked the lion cub off the cushion, into a deep, dark hole at the back of the sofa. Jack put his fingers down the hole. He couldn't feel the lion cub at all.

"We need rescue vehicles," he said and reached for his fire engine and ambulance. "Nee-naw, nee-naw, nee-naw!" First the fire engine went down the hole, then the ambulance.

Jack clambered to the other end of the sofa. He found another hole. Maybe the lion cub had slipped in between.

He put his fingers down the hole. It felt dusty inside. He pulled out a penny and a hair clip with a dolphin on it.

"There's undersea treasure down here," he said to his toys. "It's a dolphin's cave. Let's explore."

All the other toys went into the dolphin's cave, even Elephant. Jack looked around the sofa. "Now, who's going to pull up the treasure chest?"

But there were no toys left.

They'd all gone down that hole.

The sofa was empty.

Only the old penny lay on the cushion.

Jack thought for a moment. He went up to his bedroom and found a pencil. He came back and tried to poke the toys out but he only poked them further in, and he lost the pencil too.

Then Jack went to the cupboard under the stairs where Dad kept his torch. Jack climbed back onto the sofa and shone the torch down one of the holes. He could just see a wheel and a bit of giraffe. But he still couldn't reach them.

At last Jack decided he needed some help. He went into the kitchen. Mum was talking on the phone and Lily was crying because she had fallen over. Dad gave Lily a cuddle and tried to cheer her up, but Lily cried even more.

No one heard Jack ask for help. No one even noticed him. So Jack went out into the garden where it was quiet and climbed to the top of the climbing frame to play pirates.

That evening when Jack and Lily were asleep in bed, Mum and Dad sat down on the sofa to watch television.

"Ouch!" said Mum and nearly spilt her coffee.

"Ouch!" said Dad and jumped right up.

They tipped the sofa upside down and to their surprise out tumbled Jack's zoo, the dolphin hair clip, the fierce lion cub, the burglar sports car, the fire engine, the ambulance, the elephant and a pencil!

But busy, tired Jack had forgotten all about them. He was fast asleep and dreaming. Who knows what he would play tomorrow?

The New Shoes

Jack's feet had been growing fast and his shoes were feeling tight.

Mum knelt down and pressed the toes of Jack's sandals. His feet were a bit squashed up at the end.

"These are too small now. You need new shoes and probably new slippers and welly boots too," she said.

Lily sat down and pressed the toes of her shoes, just like Mum had done.

"Too small," she said and shook her head. Then do you know what she did? She tugged at the sticky straps, took the shoes off and put them in the waste paper basket!

"You might need new shoes, Lily," said Mum, "but I'm afraid I'm not sure about new slippers and welly boots as well. Perhaps we can find you a pair of Jack's old slippers and those froggy boots he used to wear."

Lily had never seen the froggy boots and Jack had forgotten what they looked like. So Mum fetched them from the cupboard. Each green boot had big goggle eyes and a wide smiling mouth. Lily sat down and pulled them on all by herself, but when she stood up they looked funny.

"They're on the wrong feet, silly," said Jack.

Mum swapped the boots over and they fitted perfectly. Lily was very happy. She tried to walk around bent over so that she could see the eyes better but she kept bumping into things.

"Why don't you go into the garden and do some frog jumping with Jack," said Mum.

"I'll take you into town to buy some new shoes later," Dad said. It was Saturday morning so he wasn't at work.

Jack was pleased. He liked going in Dad's car because there were sometimes half-eaten bars of chocolate in it. When it was time to leave Jack helped Dad take the car seats out of Mum's car and put them into his.

On the way Dad switched on the radio but he couldn't find any music he liked, so they played 'I spy' instead. When they got to town Dad put Lily in her pushchair and they walked to the shops.

The shoe shop was enormous. All the children's shoes were upstairs. Jack had to take a ticket so the shop ladies would know who was next. While they were waiting Lily noticed a big fish tank in the corner. Lily loved fish. She pressed her nose up to the glass and watched them swim.

"Let's have a look at the shoes while we're waiting," said Dad.

The shop had shoes of every colour. Some had buckles, some had laces, some were fixed together with sticky straps. There was a pair the same as Jack's old shoes. There were some with glitter and sparkles, some with pictures on the toes, even spotty and stripy sandals. Lily picked up a fluffy slipper with a rabbit's head on the front, but Jack didn't want those. He chose slippers with trains on.

"We'll have to see what they have in your size," said Dad. When the number on their ticket was called Dad waved his hand. A smiling lady came over. "Hello. Who's having new shoes today?" she said.

"We both are," replied Jack. He liked the shoe shop lady's face. "I need shoes and slippers and welly boots, but Lily only needs shoes," he said.

"Shall we do her first then?" The shoe shop lady fetched a special foot measure. Lily had to stand on the measure and the lady tightened a strap across her foot.

"This measures how wide your foot is," she explained. Then she measured how long Lily's foot was. Lily kept scrunching her toes up, which made it very difficult.

Dad looked at the little girls' shoes with Lily and she picked up the sparkly pair.

"Not those, Lily," said Dad. But she wouldn't let go. Dad showed her some blue ones, but Lily shook her head. Just then a big girl came up with her mum.

"Can I try on that sparkly shoe?" she said.

Dad looked at Lily. Lily looked at Dad. He held out his hand. "Give it to me, please, Lily. It's not the right shoe for us."

Lily hid the shoe behind her back. She looked at everyone looking at her. Then she dropped the sparkly shoe and grabbed the rabbit slipper instead.

Dad had a feeling that buying shoes for Lily wasn't going to be easy. "I think we'd better do Jack first," he said.

The shoe shop lady measured Jack's feet and went to the storeroom to see what she had in his size. She came back with two boxes. Jack liked the green pair she showed him but he didn't like the brown ones. Jack didn't like brown. So they tried the green shoes first.

"Let me see you walk in these," said the shoe shop lady. Jack walked across the room and back again. The shoes fitted perfectly.

"That was easy," said Dad. "We'll have the green ones, please."

Next Jack asked for the train slippers but his size was sold out. Jack was disappointed. The only slippers left were brown, but Jack didn't like brown. Dad said he had to have them. Jack started to feel grumpy.

"Never mind about the slippers, Jack," said Dad. "Look at these." He picked up a pair of blue welly boots in the shape of an elephant's head with a long trunk and tusks. Jack loved them straight away.

"We call them Elly-Wellies," said the shoe shop lady.

"Can I wear them home?" asked Jack.

"All right," said Dad. "Maybe we'll stop at the park on the way home and find you some puddles to jump in."

Meanwhile Lily had been sitting quietly, cuddling the rabbit slipper and watching everything. She watched the fish tank and the other children trying on shoes, and she watched the shoe shop ladies going in and out of the store room with their boxes.

But when Dad looked around for Lily, she was nowhere to be seen.

"Oh no!" said Dad. "Where's Lily? Has anyone seen a little girl in a purple dress and green froggy boots?"
No one had. Dad rushed downstairs.
Lily wasn't there. He looked out into
the street. There were hundreds of
people doing their shopping.
Where could Lily be?

Suddenly one of the shop ladies went into the store room and saw a little girl sitting, smiling, in the middle of a pile of shoes and empty boxes. Lily had a very large sparkly shoe on one foot and a rabbit slipper on the other.

Dad was so pleased to find her that he let Lily have a pair of sparkly shoes after all.

"I suppose you did have to wait a long time, Pickle," he said.

Lily liked being called Pickle. She liked going shopping with Dad. And she liked, she absolutely loved, her new shoes.

The shop lady put Jack's old shoes, his new slippers and Lily's froggy boots into a big bag and all the shop ladies waved goodbye as they left.

When it was bedtime Lily wouldn't take her new shoes off. At last, when she was fast asleep, Mum crept into her bedroom and carefully slipped them off. Then she tucked a tiny teddy into each one and put them beside Lily's bed. Lily just sighed and rolled over. I wonder what she was dreaming about?

Bird Pudding

It was a wintry Thursday afternoon. Jack and Lily had gone to Grandma and Grandad's house as usual, while Mum went shopping.

Grandma had taken Lily to visit her next-door neighbour who had a new baby. Lily loved babies and Grandma had knitted a tiny jacket and hat as a present to keep the baby warm.

Jack and Grandad stayed at home. They looked out of the window into the frosty, white garden. A robin hopped onto the frozen bird bath.

"He's looking at us," said Jack.

"He needs a drink," said Grandad.

So they put on their coats and went outside. Grandad broke the ice with a stone and Jack poured some fresh water in.

"What does he eat?" asked Jack.

"Bird pudding," replied Grandad.

"How does he make it?" asked Jack.

Grandad laughed. "He doesn't make it, we do! Come on, I'll show you."

In the kitchen Grandad fetched a saucepan and a packet of suet. Jack opened the box. The suet was like little white worms.

"Pour it in," said Grandad.

Jack liked helping Grandad. He always had time to explain things to Jack and show him what to do.

"Now, hmmm," Grandad peered into the fridge. "A bit of old cheese, that's what we need." He asked Jack to bring the big mixing bowl from the cupboard. Jack carried it very carefully.

Then Grandad opened the biscuit tin. "Take that last one for yourself, Jack, and tip all the crumbs into the bowl." Grandad added the cheese and a handful of sultanas.

"Here are some nuts left over from Christmas."

"I'm not allowed to eat nuts," said Jack.

"No, but Robin and his friends will love them," said Grandad. "That reminds me . . ." He pulled Grandma's cake tin down from the shelf. Inside was some Christmas cake. "We won this in a raffle," said Grandad. "It's not as good as your Grandma's home-made." He pulled a face as if he had eaten something horrible. "Not enough big fat raisins for me!"

Jack enjoyed crumbling that into the bowl. He ate some too and he didn't think it was horrible at all.

When the mixture was ready Grandad melted the suet and Jack stirred it into the bowl. "It's glueing everything together," cried Jack.

"Good," said Grandad. "We'll put it into some plastic cups and then into the fridge to set."

Jack got very messy indeed spooning out the mixture, but Grandad didn't mind. He just winked and handed Jack a cloth. "If it's not messy it's not fun," he said. "But I think we'd better tidy up now."

Jack looked out of the window for the robin but he wasn't there. "He's gone away," said Jack sadly.

"Oh no," said Grandad. "This garden is his home, his territory. He isn't far away, you'll see. Let's have a story while we wait."

Jack ran upstairs into the spare bedroom. Beside the bed was a little bookcase with picture books and colouring books, a packet of Snap cards and some jigsaws. Grandma and Grandad kept these specially for Jack and Lily. Jack chose a book and took it to Grandad who was sitting in the window chair. Jack called it the story chair. Grandad always used different voices for everyone in a story. Jack thought he was the best reader.

By the time they had finished, the puddings had set hard. Grandad turned on the hot tap and twirled a pudding underneath. It melted just enough to pop out of its cup. Jack carried the pudding and Grandad carried Jack out into the garden to the bird table. In the middle was a nail sticking up. Jack pushed the pudding onto the nail and gave it a wiggle to make sure it wouldn't fall off.

"Now," said Grandad, "it feels like time for a cup of tea to me."

Grandad and Jack sat by the window with their cup of tea and beaker of squash. Grandad showed Jack another book. It was about birds. Jack looked at the pictures and found some that he knew – a blackbird, a blue tit and a seagull.

They watched to see who would come into the garden. Jack kept very still in case he frightened the birds away. Before long the robin flew onto the bird table. He looked straight at Grandad and Jack, then he started to peck at the pudding.

"He's eating it!" cried Jack. "He likes it!"

"Of course," said Grandad and he shook Jack's hand. "You see, we're very good cooks!"

Lily's Words

Sometimes Jack liked to play with his toys. Sometimes he liked to rush about and make lots of noise. But every now and then he liked to sit still and quiet by himself, just looking at his books.

One afternoon Jack was sitting on the sofa looking at a big book with lots of stories in it. Mum and Jack had chosen it together from the library. He couldn't quite read but he looked very hard at everything in the pictures and tried to work out what the stories were about.

Suddenly Mittens ran into the sitting room. Lily followed with her hairbrush. She wanted to brush the kitten's fur, but Mittens kept running away!

When Lily saw Jack with the book she dropped the brush and climbed onto the sofa beside him.

"Oh, Lily," sighed Jack. He didn't want her to disturb him. Lily wriggled as close as she could. She thought he would read her a story.

"Lily, I can't read you a story," said Jack.

But Lily pointed to a picture in the book. "Cat!" she said. It was a cat.

"That's right," said Jack. "Where's the cow?"

"There!" said Lily, pointing at the cow.

Jack chose something smaller in the picture. "Where's the bird?"

Lily looked for a moment. "There!" she said and pointed to the bird.

"That's right, clever girl," said Jack, just like Mum did. Lily reached across and turned over the page for some more. Jack decided to tell her his own made-up story about the pictures. It was a story about a bear who lost his hat. Lily sat very still and listened. She thought it was the real story. Now Jack didn't mind Lily squashing up close to him. He liked her smell of strawberry jam. He felt very grown-up telling her a story.

At the end Lily pointed to the picture. "Bear, there!" she said.

"And where's the hat?" asked Jack.

Lily tapped herself on the head and said "Hair!"

Jack laughed. "Bear, there, hair," he said. "It's a poem, Lily."

"Bear, there, hair," said Lily. She didn't know what a poem was but she liked the sound of the words.

"Bear, there, hair . . . bear, bear, there."

Jack and Lily said their poem loudly, over and over again. They slid off the sofa and marched around the room.

"BEAR, THERE, HAIR! BEAR, BEAR, THERE!"

Jack stamped into the kitchen where Dad was washing up.

"Lily has made a poem," he said. "Bear, there, hair!"

Dad smiled. "It certainly rhymes," he said. "I can see another word for your poem," and he pointed at the fruit bowl.

"It's pear . . ." said Jack, "and chair. Bear, there, pear, chair!"

But just at that moment Lily appeared in the doorway. She was carrying the big book by its pages.

"Oh, oh," she said.

Dad and Jack stopped and looked. They knew exactly what Lily's 'oh, oh,' always meant. Sure enough Lily had had an accident. One of the pages of the book was torn.

Dad frowned. He dried his hands and took the book. He closed it and showed Lily how to carry a book properly.

"I expect I can mend that with some sticky tape," said Dad. "But I'll have to explain what happened to the library lady. Maybe you can teach Lily a few more words for her poem, Jack."

Jack looked around the kitchen. "What are they?" he asked.

Can you guess what they were?

Dad sat down and lifted Lily onto his lap. "They are 'tear'," he said, "and 'take care!' "

Jack's Mouse

When Jack was born Grandma and Grandad gave him a present. It was a blue mouse with a long tail, round soft ears and a smile. Now Jack had lots of toys; bears, rabbits and two tigers. But he still loved Mouse because only Mouse had a smile.

Mouse also had a label stitched to his leg. Jack liked to stroke the silky label when he went to sleep. Every night he cuddled Mouse in bed. Whenever he was unhappy, holding Mouse made him feel better.

One day Jack noticed that Mouse's label was torn and ragged. He ran into the kitchen hugging Mouse tight.

"Look, his label has gone," he said sadly.

Mum was busy feeding Mittens but she knelt down to look at Mouse. Sure enough he had been hugged and stroked so much that only a thread of his label was left.

"He's still smiling," said Mum.

"He's being brave," said Jack. "I think it hurts him really."

Just then the telephone rang. It was Grandma. Mum talked to her for a long time. Jack got fed up waiting. He took Mouse into his bedroom to put a bandage on him. But he didn't have a bandage so he put him in a sock instead.

Lily was playing in her bedroom. She had pulled some toys out of the cupboard and was making them kiss each other. She made the rag doll kiss the wooden elephant and the panda kiss the knitted scarecrow. Then Lily kissed each one herself.

Suddenly she heard Jack, and went to see what he was doing.

Jack was busy with Mouse and he didn't notice Lily come in. Lily saw the sock drawer was open and do you know what she did? She started to pull all the socks out of the drawer and throw them up in the air. Jack liked Lily's games. Before you could say 'snowballs' they were both hurling socks at each other. When Mum came in a blue pair whizzed right over her shoulder.

"What's this? A sockstorm!" said Mum. "Put them all back, please."

"Oh no . . ." groaned Jack. He didn't like putting things away. "Lily started it," he said.

"Well, I don't suppose these socks are going to jump back into the drawer by themselves . . ." said Mum. "Wait here, I'll be back in a minute." And she went off downstairs to the kitchen. When she came back she made Jack and Lily stay outside the bedroom door while she went in.

"I expect she's putting them back for us," whispered Jack to Lily. "She's very kind. Can you say 'kind', Lily?"

"Mummy kind," said Lily.

"That's right," said Jack.

But Mum wasn't putting the socks back at all. When she opened the door they were still lying all over the floor.

"It's a treasure hunt," she said. "Some of the socks have treasure inside, so look carefully as you put each one away."

Jack cheered. He hoped the treasure was something to eat. And in the second sock he picked up there was a little cheese biscuit. Before long all the socks were put away and Lily's face was smiling and sticky.

While Mum was washing Lily's face the doorbell rang. She asked Jack to open the door.

"It's Grandma!" said Jack and he gave her a hug.

Grandma came in with a big basket. "I heard there was a brave Mouse here who needed some help."

Jack had forgotten all about Mouse. He suddenly felt sad again. "Mouse had a silky label but it's been hugged away," he said.

"Now I won't be able to go to sleep, and Mouse will be unhappy forever."

"Oh dear," said Grandma, taking off her coat. "We can't have that, can we. Let's see what we can do."

Jack ran to fetch Mouse while Grandma made herself comfortable in the armchair and put on her glasses. She put the big basket down beside her. When he came back Jack took off the sock bandage and gave Mouse to Grandma.

"You've looked after Mouse very well," she said. "See, he's still smiling. I'm sure we can do something about his problem." She lifted the basket onto her knee. Jack and Lily peeped in. It was a sewing basket. Inside were lots of reels of coloured cotton, scraps of cloth, a pin cushion, packets of needles, scissors, safety pins and buttons.

First Grandma pulled out a bundle of cotton reels. "I found this the other day. I think I must have made it for Mummy when she was a little girl. Maybe Lily would like to play with it while we're busy," she said.

The cotton reels were threaded together to make a long snake with a red felt tongue and shiny green eyes.

Lily loved it. She trailed it in and out of the chair legs. When Mum came in with a cup of tea for Grandma she was surprised.

"That's my Jake the Snake!" she said and she sat down to play with Lily.

"Now Jack," said Grandma, "look inside my coat pocket and bring me what you find."

Jack felt excited because he knew a surprise was going to happen. He found an envelope and gave it to Grandma.

"Hold out your hand," she said and tipped something out.

Jack gasped. There in his hand was a bright silky label.

"I cut this off a new bath towel I bought yesterday," said Grandma. "If Mouse likes it we could stitch it on." She pulled a box out of her basket. Inside were rolls of coloured ribbon. "Maybe he'd like some ribbon too."

Jack chose a golden yellow ribbon that was especially silky and gave Grandma a hug.

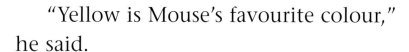

"Yellow is Mouse's favourite colour," he said.

Grandma got to work with her needle and thread. Before long Mouse had a new label on one leg, a yellow ribbon on the other and a bow around his neck. Jack was so pleased he danced with Mouse around the room. "Now he's really smiling," said Jack.

"And so are you!" said Mum.

Bedtime

Do you have a story before you go to sleep? Jack and Lily love bedtime stories.

One evening, when they were in their pyjamas, Jack and Lily scrambled onto the sofa to have a story as usual. Mum brought a cup of warm milk for Lily who sat on her lap and Jack tucked himself close beside them so he could see the pictures.

Lily always chose her story first and every evening for two weeks she had chosen the same one. It was called *Quacky Duck.* No matter how often she heard it, Lily wanted *Quacky Duck.* She knew the story so well that she could join in with the words as Mum read.

One of the pages had been repaired with a piece of sticky tape which Lily liked to stroke as she listened, because it was so smooth. At the end of the story she looked at all the pictures again and kissed the ducklings. After two weeks Jack knew the story off by heart as well, but it was funny so he didn't mind too much.

When all the ducklings were kissed it was time to go upstairs. Mum carried Lily, and while Jack went into his bedroom to choose a storybook Mum tucked her in. She snuggled under the blankets and hugged her Puppy-lamb. Mum quietly sang a song.

At the end of the song Lily crawled out of the blankets and sat up.

"More!" she said. Mum tucked her in all over again and sang a very short song this time. Lily smiled a cheeky smile.

But before she had time to wriggle out of the blankets Mum said "No more," firmly and kissed Lily goodnight.

Lily's smile turned into a yawn. "More, Mummy, more . . ." She sighed sleepily, but Mum switched off the light and left Lily to sing to herself.

Meanwhile Jack had found a bedtime story. He started to choose which toys he wanted on his pillow. Often this took quite a long time. Mouse always slept beside him but the others changed. One night Jack might want his tigers, another night he might only want his tiny teddies, but he always put them in just the right place.

Jack loved to hear Mum singing to Lily in her room next door. He knew it meant that she would soon be coming in to read to him.

Sure enough Mum came in with Jack's bedtime drink.
She put it on the little cupboard beside his bed. The
cupboard was painted with tigers chasing each other's tails
round and round. Sometimes Dad would make up a bedtime
story about those tigers running right off the cupboard and
all through the house!

Mum put Jack's clothes away and sat on his bed to read
him a story.

"What have you chosen tonight?" she said.

"I want this one about the old-fashioned car please,"
said Jack.

Now it was his turn to climb onto Mum's lap.

After the story Jack always asked for another one.

"You're just as bad as your sister wanting more songs," said
Mum giving him a hug. But it was too late for more stories.

"Can I have one for the morning?" asked Jack. Mum let him choose another book to look at when he woke up in the morning. Jack put it on the cupboard and hopped into bed.

After the story Mum and Jack always had a little chat about the day. It was their special time together. Sometimes they laughed about the funny things that Lily had done and sometimes Jack asked Mum about difficult things he didn't understand, such as where rain comes from, or how aeroplanes fly.

"What are we going to do tomorrow?" said Jack.

"Tomorrow is Grandad's birthday," said Mum. "We'll make him a birthday card in the morning and then he's coming here for tea with Grandma."

"Will there be a birthday cake?" asked Jack.

"Of course," said Mum. "You can help me make it."

"And hundreds of candles?" said Jack, yawning.

"Hundreds!" said Mum.

Last of all Jack and Mum said thank you for the day. No matter what had happened during the day they always found lots to say thank you for.

"We'd better say thank you for Grandad," said Jack.

"And thank you for Grandma," said Mum.

"Thank you for my new felt pens," said Jack.

"And for a sunny day," said Mum. "Thank you for the man at the shop who helped me pack the shopping."

"Thank you for firemen," said Jack, who'd seen a fire engine on the way home from the shop.

"Thank you for Daddy and Lily and Jack," said Mum.

"And thank you for Mum," said Jack.

Mum gave Jack a kiss, tucked him in and switched off the light. Then she opened his door, not too much and not too little, but just so he could see the light on in the hall, and Jack went to sleep thinking of birthday cake.